Standing inside the gates of the children's prison, Jacob Two-Two stared up into the menacing face of the warden—the dreaded Hooded Fang.

"Remove this prisoner to the lowest, dampest dungeon," growled The Hooded Fang. "And put him on a diet of stale bread and water."

Poor Jacob Two-Two—only two plus two plus two years old and a prisoner of The Hooded Fang. What had he done to deserve such terrible punishment? The worst crime of all— insulting a grownup.

Jacob's future seems bleak indeed. But though he is small and young he is far from helpless, and when the Infamous Two come to his aid, Child Power triumphs.

Jacob Two-Two's ordeal and rescue is the substance and delight of this marvelously funny story—a first book for children by the well-known novelist, Mordecai Richler.

JACOB TWO-TWO
MEETS
THE HOODED FANG

JACOB TWO-TWO
MEETS
THE HOODED FANG

---

by MORDECAI RICHLER

Illustrated by
FRITZ WEGNER

McClelland and Stewart Limited

For DANIEL,
NOAH,
EMMA,
MARFA,
and JACOB

JACOB TWO-TWO
MEETS
THE HOODED FANG

1

ONCE THERE WAS A BOY called Jacob Two-Two. He was two plus two plus two years old. He had two ears and two eyes and two arms and two feet and two shoes. He also had two older sisters, Emma and Marfa, and two older brothers, Daniel and Noah. And they all lived in a rambling old house on Kingston Hill in England.

Most days Jacob Two-Two was happy, but other days, bad days, he was very sad. On bad days he saw that all the other children in the house were taller and much more capable than he was. His two older brothers, and even his two older sisters, could ride two-wheel bicycles, dial a telephone number, whistle, do joined-up writing, play checkers, and catch a ball.

Mind you, life was becoming more tolerable. Once, Jacob Two-Two couldn't even reach the front doorbell. Only two years ago, when he was a mere two times two years old, Jacob Two-Two didn't even know what a day was, where yes-

terday had gone, and when tomorrow would come. Waking
up one morning, he had asked his mother, "Is this tomorrow?
Is this tomorrow?"

"No, darling, it's today."

"But when you tucked me in at night, you said when I
got up *this* day would be tomorrow. You promised! You
promised!"

"That was yesterday."

"You said it was today."

"It was, and then *this* was going to be tomorrow."

"But you just said this day is today too. You just said . . ."

"Oh, Jacob," his mother had said, kissing him, "some-
times you're too much."

4

Even though he was now two plus two plus two years old and knew more, plenty more, Jacob Two-Two was still not allowed to count sheets for the laundry or cross the street by himself; neither could he run errands for his mommy and daddy, like his older brothers and sisters. He could now pour milk into his cereal bowl without spilling some, but he still couldn't cut a slice of bread that wasn't a foot thick on one end and thin as a sheet of paper on the other. True, he was now allowed to sit in a big chair at the kitchen table, but what good was it when he could hardly see over his dinner plate and his feet didn't touch the floor but dangled foolishly? And if he lost his temper over this or other injustices and threw a punch at Daniel or Emma, they didn't even holler or hit back. They merely giggled.

One day when everybody in the house had something absorbing to do, Jacob Two-Two wandered into his big brother's bedroom.

"Out," shouted Daniel, "I'm doing my homework."

His sister Marfa was curled up on the sofa in the study watching wrestling on television.

"You can't stay in here," she said.

"Why?" asked Jacob Two-Two. "Why?"

"Because the wrestlers are doing scary things and you're still a baby and it will give you nightmares and you'll wet your bed."

"I won't," said Jacob Two-Two. "I won't."

"Look," said Marfa, pointing at the wrestler on the screen, "that's The Hooded Fang, and he's going to jump out of the TV set any minute and chew you to bits."

"I'm not frightened," said Jacob Two-Two, retreating.

In the garden, under the shelter of the copper beech tree, he found his brother Noah and his sister Emma were at it again. Dressed up, disguised, they were playing their game of pretend. Noah was dangling from the tree. He had a plastic dagger between his teeth and a big towel draped over his shoulders like a cape. "Okay, Shapiro," he shouted, "come out and fight!"

Emma raced out of her tent, waving a wooden sword. "Say your prayers, O'Toole," she snarled, "because here I come!"

As Noah swung to the ground and Emma charged, Jacob Two-Two jumped between them. "Can I play?" he asked. "Can I play?"

"Oh, no," moaned Noah. "Now you've gone and spoiled everything!"

"Then I'll be on your side," said Jacob Two-Two to his sister. "I'll help you. I'll help you."

"Oh, Jacob," she said, "you're too little to help anybody."

"Our game's too complicated for you."

"I want to play," said Jacob Two-Two. "I want to play."

"Hey," said Noah, pointing at the kitchen window, "listen, Mommy's calling you."

Jacob Two-Two found his mother in the kitchen. "Did you call me?" he asked. "Did you call me?"

"No, dear."

Jacob Two-Two didn't ask if he could help cook the dinner. He knew his mother would smile and say he was too little, just as he was too little to go to a real school, like the one his brothers went to. And, more than anything, Jacob Two-Two longed to go to a real school, even though Noah had warned him they had punishment cells there, dark and gloomy, with double-locked doors, and that naughty boys ultimately had to appear before a judge. At a real school, Noah had also said, good boys were served chips with red wine for lunch, followed by ice cream and cigars.

"Now you run off and play," said Jacob Two-Two's mother. "I'll call you when dinner's ready."

His brothers and sisters didn't want him. His mother didn't need him. So Jacob Two-Two went to find his father. He was lying on the living room sofa reading the newspaper.

"I want to run an errand," said Jacob Two-Two. "I want to run an errand."

"You're still too small," said his father.

"No, I'm not. I'm not!" said Jacob Two-Two. And, suddenly, he burst into tears.

"All right, then." His father dug into his pocket for some coins. "Go to Mr. Cooper, the greengrocer, two doors down the street, and get me two pounds of firm, red tomatoes."

2

JACOB TWO-TWO RAN OFF, just a little frightened because this was his first errand, and Emma had warned him that Mr. Cooper, the greengrocer, was two-faced. He was nice to children as long as their parents were with them. He pinched their cheeks and offered them grapes. But if a child came into his shop alone, he made him wait until all the big people had been served. Emma said Mr. Cooper was sour as a lemon.

Jacob Two-Two clutched his coins as he entered Mr. Cooper's shop. He saw that the greengrocer was pear-shaped, his brown hair cut short, like a coconut. His eyes were small as orange seeds, but his ears big as cauliflower leaves. His nose was red and veined as a beet, and his stomach stuck out like a sack of potatoes.

"What do you want?" asked Mr. Cooper.

"I want two pounds of firm, red tomatoes. I want two pounds of firm, red tomatoes."

Mr. Cooper frowned. He was insulted. For he had no way

of knowing that Jacob Two-Two said everything two times, because what with so many people in his house, two parents, two older brothers and two older sisters, nobody ever heard him the first time.

"There's no need to chew your cabbage twice in here," said Mr. Cooper.

"But I'm Jacob Two-Two. I'm two plus two plus two years old. And, if you please, I want two pounds of firm, red tomatoes. Two pounds of firm, red tomatoes."

"You stop making fun of me," said Mr. Cooper, winking

at his other customers, all of them big people, "or I'll call the police."

And just then Mr. Cooper did in fact see the policeman passing on his rounds and summoned him inside.

"What is it, Mr. Cooper?" asked the policeman.

"I'm being mocked," said Mr. Cooper. All the big people in the shop laughed. "By this one," the greengrocer added, pointing a finger as long as a carrot at Jacob Two-Two.

The policeman looked down at Jacob Two-Two. "What is it, boy?"

Terrified, Jacob Two-Two replied: "All I want, if you please, is two pounds of firm, red tomatoes. All I want is two pounds of firm, red tomatoes."

Mr. Cooper stamped his foot. He beat his fist against his forehead. "I demand justice. This exasperating little boy," he insisted, "must be charged with insulting behavior to a big person."

The policeman, holding back his laughter, took a step toward Jacob Two-Two. But Jacob Two-Two, his heart thumping, ducked and flew out of the shop.

"Hey," Mr. Cooper called after him, "come back here. We were only teasing you."

Jacob Two-Two had already cleared the corner and was racing down the hill and into Richmond Park, flying past the high iron gates that were shut after dark, like prison bars. He ran and ran, avoiding the pond, which Marfa had warned him was full of crocodiles and snakes. He ran with his head down, keeping a sharp eye out for poisonous snakes, a threat which Noah protected him against for only a penny a week.

Finally, he sank to the grass, out of breath.

Only then did he notice the fog beginning to settle, closing in on him. Shivering just a little, Jacob Two-Two rubbed his eyes.

3

THE VERY NEXT THING HE KNEW, Jacob Two-Two was double-locked into a gloomy dark cell beneath the towering court house. Suddenly, the cell door clanged open and a fat police-man thrust somebody toward him, saying, "Jacob Two-Two, it is my duty to inform you that you and your visitor are, according to the strict letter of the law, allowed one hour to-gether . . . *before facing the judge.*"

The visitor who had come tumbling into the cell was quite the scruffiest, skinniest, and most untidy man Jacob Two-Two had ever seen. With tangled gray hair and weepy blue eyes. His shirt collar was frayed, and his tie soup-stained. His suit was rumpled. His shoes were scuffed, the laces broken. Beaming at Jacob Two-Two, he declared: "Meet your barrister, Louis Loser."

"Oh, I'm very pleased to meet you, Mr. Loser," said Jacob Two-Two two times.

"Are you, *really?*" replied Louis Loser, astonished.

"Yes. But what's a barrister? What's a barrister?"

"Your protector in court."

"Oh, but I haven't got any money, Mr. Loser. I couldn't afford to pay you."

"Of course not," said Louis Loser impatiently. "If you could afford it, you'd pay me to stay home in bed."

"Do people pay you *not* to protect them in court?" asked Jacob Two-Two twice.

"Only if they can afford it."

"Oooo," groaned Jacob Two-Two. "Oooo."

"You mustn't worry, my boy. The truth is, I've never won a case in my life, and that can't go on forever," pleaded Louis Loser, tears rolling down his cheeks, "can it?"

"No," said Jacob Two-Two, "no." Adding hopefully, "Maybe this could be your lucky day at last."

"*Lucky day?*" Louis Loser thrust out his puny chest. "My dear boy," he said, obviously insulted, "don't you realize that you are looking at *the* Louis Loser? When I set out on a picnic, it rains. If I'm invited to a party, I turn up on the wrong night. I can't sharpen a pencil without breaking it or slice bread evenly."

"Oh," said Jacob Two-Two, enormously pleased to discover that he wasn't the only one. "And what happens when you turn on the television?"

"The picture's fuzzy. It flips, it flops. Or the screen is buried in snow."

"Me, too," said Jacob Two-Two, enthralled, "me, too. I'm so pleased that you are going to protect me in court."

"Well, thank you!" said Louis Loser, and then he told Jacob Two-Two a story. "Once," he began, "I very nearly had a lucky day. I went into court with what seemed like an air-tight case. Impossible to lose, even for Louis Loser. My client was out taking the air one evening when three ruffians attacked him. They took his wallet, they stole his watch, and beat him up very badly. Fortunately, a police car just happened to come along, and the ruffians were caught red-handed. In court, they confessed to everything. And my client, I must say, was a most touching sight, bandaged from head to toe and standing on crutches. All we claimed were damages."

"Did you win? Did you win?"

"Certainly not."

"What happened?" asked Jacob Two-Two. "What happened?"

"How was I to know," said Louis Loser, sniffling, "that my client would turn out to be an internationally famous bank robber, Public Enemy Number One in ten countries. The ruffians who beat and robbed him were each given a ten thousand pound reward for their troubles. My client was sent to prison for life. And the judge booted me out of court, saying only a rotter would stoop to defend such a notorious criminal."

The policeman banged on the cell door, warning them they had only another five minutes together. A chill ran through Jacob Two-Two as he was suddenly reminded of his own impending trial. "How will you defend me?" asked Jacob Two-Two, terrified. "How will you defend me?"

Louis Loser, deep in thought, paced the cell. "I will not plead extenuating circumstances; neither will I claim a mistrial. It wouldn't do any good to ask for a change of venue or challenge the jury's competence . . ."

"Then what will you do?" asked Jacob Two-Two. "What will you do, Mr. Loser?"

"I've got it!" exclaimed Louis Loser triumphantly. "*I'll cry.*"

"But that won't help."

"Of course not. But, in my cases, nothing does," said Louis

Loser with immense pride. "Come on, my boy. It's time to go."

Jacob Two-Two took Louis Loser's hand. "I have faith in you, Mr. Loser," he said, his voice wobbly.

Even as tears streamed down his cheeks, Louis Loser beamed. "In that event," he said, "we can't lose."

"How come?" asked Jacob Two-Two, delighted. "How come?"

"Because if you have faith in me, I'm going to plead insanity on your behalf. You're nuts, my boy. Positively crackers."

4

WITHIN MINUTES, JACOB TWO-TWO stood before the judge in the children's court.

Nowhere among the jeering spectators, many of them customers of the greengrocer, could Jacob Two-Two see Daniel, Noah, Emma, Marfa, or his mother and father. But had he looked a little more carefully, he would have seen two mysterious little people. Midgets, maybe. Wearing beards, dark glasses, and trenchcoats, they were holding notebooks, pens poised.

The children's judge, Mr. Justice Rough, wore a white powdered wig and a long black gown. "I see here," he growled, "that you are charged with insulting behavior, not to another brat—I mean, child—but, good heavens, *to a big person*. This is serious. Extremely serious. If you got away with it, it could only lead to more monstrous crimes, like hiding comics under your pillow or peeing without lifting the seat." Here Mr.

19

Justice Rough paused and knit his fierce brows. "Once and for all, children must be taught—"

"—THAT BIG PEOPLE ARE NEVER, NEVER WRONG," all the big people in the court shouted back.

"If they punish you," Mr. Justice Rough called out, "it's—"

"—FOR YOUR OWN GOOD," the big people called back.

"And it hurts them—" Mr. Justice Rough continued.

"—MORE THAN IT HURTS YOU," the big people replied.

Then the clerk of the court stepped up to Jacob Two-Two. "How do you plead, you little nit?" he asked.

"Oh, what's the difference," the foreman of the jury hollered, "he's guilty."

"I object," said Louis Loser in a small voice.

"*You what?*" bellowed Mr. Justice Rough.

"I didn't say a word," said Louis Loser, shriveling.

"Now, then," said Mr. Justice Rough, banging his gavel, demanding silence. "I must remind all of you that we are here to see that this lad gets a fair trial. Jacob Two-Two," he continued, turning to the accused, "I should warn you that in this court, as in life, little people are considered guilty, unless they can prove themselves innocent, which is just short of impossible."

The big people in court whistled. They roared with laughter. They stamped their feet and shouted, "Hear! Hear!"

"Well, then," said the clerk of the court, "let's get on with it. How do you plead?"

Jacob Two-Two turned to Louis Loser, looking for guidance. His protector was hiding under his desk, shaking with sobs. So taking a deep breath, Jacob Two-Two said, "Why with all respect, sir, I plead innocent. Why, with all respect, sir, I plead innocent."

"That's abominable! It's most inconsiderate," said Mr. Justice Rough, "for I am the busiest of busy judges. In an average day here I deal with desperadoes, swindlers, bubble-gum smugglers, chocolate bar addicts, boys who want a bigger allowance, and girls who grow out of their shoes too soon —the lot!—all of whom have one thing in common. They are rude to big people. Why, you wouldn't even exist—" sang out Mr. Justice Rough, enraged.

"—IF NOT FOR YOUR PARENTS," the big people shouted back.

"Everything you have—" continued Mr. Justice Rough.

"—YOU OWE TO US," chimed in the big people.

The courtroom began to sway around Jacob Two-Two.

"I haven't much time," said Mr. Justice Rough. "If I don't get through your case quickly, I'll be late for my afternoon nap." The judge paused; he glared at Jacob Two-Two. "If you're innocent, why are you here?"

"Because I want two pounds of firm, red tomatoes," said Jacob Two-Two. "I want two pounds of firm, red tomatoes."

"Don't mock me, boy. I heard you right the first time."

"But, your Lordship, he says almost everything two times," said the prosecutor, "and that's why he stands before you."

Mr. Justice Rough leaned toward Jacob Two-Two. "Why must you say everything two times?" he asked.

"Because," said Jacob Two-Two, pleased to be able to explain himself, "I am two plus two plus two years old. I have two ears and two eyes and two arms and two feet and two shoes. I also have two sisters and two brothers. I am the littlest. Nobody hears me the first time. They only pay attention if I say things two times. And now, your Lordship, could I have two pounds of firm, red tomatoes? Could I please,

please, have my two pounds of firm, red tomatoes?" and, he thought, swallowing hard, be allowed to go home. Oh, please.

"Are you finished, then?" asked Mr. Justice Rough.

Jacob Two-Two nodded twice.

"Thank God for *that!*" Bang, bang, went the judge's gavel. Bang, bang, again. "Wake up the jury," he demanded gruffly.

The clerk of the court shook the jury awake.

"Now, then," said Mr. Justice Rough, "you've heard the evidence. How do you find the defendant?"

"Guilty!"

"Well, if that's how you feel," said Mr. Justice Rough, rubbing his hands together gleefully, "I will now pass sentence. Jacob Two-Two, because you are an unredeemed scoundrel, a charlatan, an ingrate, and a smart aleck to boot, I hearby sentence you to two years, two months, two weeks, two days, two hours and two minutes in the darkest dungeons of the children's prison. I do this for your own good, naturally, and it hurts me more than it hurts you."

Suddenly, a bell-like voice rang out loud and clear: "*We will appeal this verdict, of course.*"

"Oh, yes," sneered Mr. Justice Rough, rocking with laughter, "and who might you be?"

Right there, right then, the two little people shed their disguises.

They flung off their beards.

They discarded their dark glasses.

They tossed away their trenchcoats.

And, lo and behold, revealed in Day-Glo blue jeans and flying golden capes, the spine-chilling emblem *Child Power* emblazoned on their chests, were the intrepid Shapiro and the fearless O'Toole.

"Take cover, everybody!"

"Look out!"

"It's the Infamous Two!"

"I am O'Toole," announced Noah, leaping on to a table.

"And I am Shapiro," proclaimed Emma, rippling her muscles for all to see.

Immediately, the two burliest policemen in court fainted. Teeth chattering, the prosecutor dived under his table. The jury, wide awake for the first time, stumbled over each other, fleeing their benches.

Shapiro, followed by O'Toole, traversed the court room, swinging from one chandelier to the next, dropping to the floor immediately before the trembling Mr. Justice Rough.

"I-I-I-I," began Mr. Justice Rough, "a-a-am a grandfather myself. I a-a-a-adore children, beautiful little people. Have a gumdrop?"

"Stuff it," said Shapiro.

"You'll be hearing from us," warned O'Toole.

5

BUT FOR ALL THEIR BIG TALK and threats, The Infamous Two did not interfere when Jacob Two-Two was carted off by two policemen to spend the night locked in the cell below the towering courthouse, before being shipped to the abominable children's prison.

Jacob Two-Two, who was used to being tucked into a warm bed surrounded by his stuffed animals, tried his best to settle down on the bare wooden board in his cold cell. Unable to sleep, he passed the time trying to decipher messages scrawled on the walls by previous prisoners. The most prominent message, printed in blood-red, warned:

BEWARE OF THE HOODED FANG

The who?, thought Jacob Two-Two, when suddenly he heard somebody at his high barred window.

"Psssst! Psssst!"

Raising himself, Jacob Two-Two saw that it was the intrepid Shapiro, accompanied by the fearless O'Toole.

"We could have rescued you," said O'Toole.

"Oh, yeah?"

"But Child Power needs your help," said Shapiro.

"Aren't I," asked Jacob Two-Two a little sarcastically, "too little to help anybody?"

"Oh no," said O'Toole.

"You must help us uncover the hidden children's prison," said Shapiro, "and rescue all the poor wretches being held there."

"But how?" asked Jacob Two-Two two times.

"Hide this secret supersonic bleeper in your ear," said O'Toole, "and we will find you, wherever you are."

So Jacob Two-Two slipped the supersonic bleeper into his ear and was still wearing it the next morning when, blindfolded, he began his long journey to the children's prison, taking a route so utterly confusing as to confound even the most ingenious of his pursuers. Accompanied by two guards wearing dark glasses, *wearing dark glasses all the time,* he traveled by car, train, bus, canoe, helicopter, ox-cart, rickshaw, stilts, dinghy, skis, submarine, flying balloon, camel, raft, dogsled, roller skates, glider and motorcycle.

Jacob Two-Two's two guards on his seemingly endless journey were called Master Fish and Mistress Fowl.

"I suppose," snarled Master Fish, "that your daddy loves you?"

"Oh, yes," replied Jacob Two-Two. "Oh, yes."

"Well, I don't, you little stinker. In fact, I think you're perfectly horrible."

Jacob Two-Two lowered his head.

"I can see," sneered Mistress Fowl, "that you're used to being treated kindly. Why, I'll bet your mother reads you a story before tucking you in at night."

Jacob Two-Two smiled in fond remembrance. He nodded twice.

"Well, you repulsive little brat, you just wait until you hear the bedtime stories we read over the loudspeaker system in the children's prison."

Jacob Two-Two loved stories. "Are they good ones?" he asked hopefully. "Are they good ones?"

"They certainly are," said Master Fish, "if you like to tremble in the dark and listen to tales of red-eyed witches."

"Or bloodthirsty vampires," said Mistress Fowl.

"Or kidnappers."

"Or monsters from outer space."

Jacob Two-Two shuddered.

"The children's prison," said Master Fish, delighted, "awaits your pleasure."

"But why," asked Jacob Two-Two, "why a prison for children?"

Master Fish was outraged. Mistress Fowl was appalled.

"Don't you think there ought to be a place," snarled Master Fish, "for little people so utterly hopeless they can't even ride a two-wheel bicycle?"

"Or dial a telephone number," sneered Mistress Fowl.

"Or count the laundry?"

"Or even cross the street by themselves?"

Jacob Two-Two swallowed his tears.

"Look here, you useless twerp, little people are always doing the wrong thing."

"Like waking up their parents at six o'clock on a Sunday morning to say the sun is out."

"Or gobbling all the peaches on the kitchen table before their elder brothers and sisters come down."

Or, Jacob Two-Two had to admit to himself, recalling the incident with a shudder, running to answer the telephone and telling Daniel's new girl friend that his brother couldn't take the call, because he was on the toilet, doing his dump.

"Admit it, clunkhead," snapped Master Fish, "how many times have you watered all the house plants only an hour after your mother had done it?"

"I was only trying to be helpful," protested Jacob Two-Two. "I was only trying to be helpful."

"Yes, certainly. But you drowned them, didn't you?"

"Ignorant little troublemaker!"

Jacob Two-Two retreated, convinced by his tormentors that there simply had to be a prison for little people as obnoxious as he was, but in his worst dreams he was not prepared for what lay ahead.

Fog, fog everywhere.

Mistress Fowl smiled. Master Fish began to whistle a happy tune. And for the very first time, they actually removed their dark glasses.

Jacob Two-Two shivered. It was so cold. As his eyes adjusted to the dim light, the first thing he made out, in the distance, were two gigantic chimney stacks, filthy gray fog billowing from both of them.

"Look," said Mistress Fowl, "we're almost there."

As they emerged from a field of tall spiky grass onto a muddy shore, Jacob Two-Two made out a sign that read:

THIS WAY TO SLIMERS' ISLE
FROM WHICH NO BRATS
RETURN

The sign pointed toward a rowboat, a leaky rowboat, and Jacob Two-Two was flung into it by his guards.

"I'll row," said Master Fish.

"I'll steer," said Mistress Fowl.

"And you, my dear," they shouted together, "will bail. *Or we might sink,*" they added, bursting into laughter.

Rusty can in hand, Jacob Two-Two bailed furiously, for the murky waters, he quickly saw, were infested with blood-thirsty sharks and slimy crocodiles, their jaws snapping hungrily. And it was no better once they reached the opposite shore, where the first thing to greet Jacob Two-Two was a slithering snake.

"Poisonous, of course," said Master Fish.

The children's prison, Jacob Two-Two learned, was built on a marshy island in the foggiest part of England, a place where the sun never shone. The only birds that ever flew over the island were buzzards, and the land could support no animal life other than gray wolverines with yellow snaggle-teeth and millions of deathwatch beetles. There were no flowers, boasted Master Fish, but nettles thrived everywhere, hiding the quicksand, added Mistress Fowl.

The prison itself, Jacob Two-Two saw, was built of clammy gray stone. As he approached, its ugly towers, choked with vines that yielded poisonous blackberries, rose gloomily into the never-ending fog.

"Home, sweet home," cried Mistress Fowl.

6

FINALLY, THEY REACHED THE GATES of the children's prison, where an enormous flashing sign proclaimed:

TREMBLE, KIDS!

SHIVER!

SHUDDER!

YOU ARE APPROACHING

THE LAIR

OF THE

HOODED FANG!

Underneath, neon blood dripped into a seething, steaming cauldron, and a perpetual laughing machine cackled *"Ho! Ho! Ho!"*

Once inside the prison, Master Fish and Mistress Fowl thrust Jacob Two-Two into the warden's lair. The warden was known as The Hooded Fang. Jacob Two-Two, looking very pale, discovered him sprawled on the floor, smelly and unshaven, sharpening his fangs by gnawing on a beef bone, a marrow bone. The Hooded Fang seized Jacob Two-Two's charge sheet, muttering to himself as he clutched it between his paws. "Mmmnnn," said The Hooded Fang, "insulting behavior to a big person, eh? We'll soon cure that, we will. What led you into such serious trouble?"

"Two pounds of firm, red tomatoes," said Jacob Two-Two, sighing. "Two pounds of firm, red tomatoes."

"Why are you saying things two times? Take me for an idiot, do you?"

"No, sir. No, sir."

"Remove this desperado to the lowest, dampest dungeon," said The Hooded Fang, "and put him on a diet of stale bread and water. My shaving water! Ho, ho, ho!"

"Can I have two slices, please?" asked Jacob Two-Two. "Can I have two slices?"

"You see," said The Hooded Fang, strutting, "he's only been here two minutes and he's begging for mercy. Am I tough! Oh, boy, I'm the toughest!" The Hooded Fang growled at Jacob Two-Two. He bared his fangs. "Shall I tell you why I hate kids more than anything in this world?"

"Please do," said Jacob Two-Two. "Please do."

The Hooded Fang dismissed Master Fish and Mistress Fowl and locked the door to his lair.

"Once," he began, "I was a star, with my own dressing room. The Hooded Fang, most hated and vile villain in all of

wrestling. Why, as I made my way from my dressing room into the arena, the boos were sufficient to raise the roof beams. And the minute I stepped into the ring, the fans pelted me with stinking fish, rotten eggs, and overripe tomatoes. Oh, it was lovely!"

"Then," said The Hooded Fang, his eyes suddenly charged with menace, "it happened. One dreadful evening in Doncaster, just as I slipped between the ropes, waiting for the eggs and fish to fly . . . *a child laughed*. A child, standing on a chair in the front row, pointed at me, laughed out loud, and said, 'He's not terrible, Daddy, he's funny!' *Funny?* Desperately, I rolled my eyes. I bared my fangs. I made menacing faces. But nobody threw anything. Not one little rotten egg. The child wouldn't stop laughing. And, before you knew it, the whole arena was convulsed. The more I growled, the louder they laughed. When my opponent entered the ring, I immediately poked my thumb into his eye, but instead of hitting back, he just fell against the ropes, roaring with laughter."

The Hooded Fang blew his nose. His head hung heavy.

"These things get around, you know. It was in the newspapers. And soon, wherever I went, all I had to do was crawl through the ropes, and the fans were laughing so hard, tears came to their eyes. *All because a child laughed*. A funny villain is no good, don't you see? No good at all."

"Oh, I'm sorry, Mr. Hooded Fang," said Jacob Two-Two. "I'm sorry."

"Are you?" asked The Hooded Fang, surprised. "Why?"

"Because you seem to be such a nice man."

"What?" roared The Hooded Fang. "How dare you! I'm not nice. I'm horrible, disgusting, mean, vicious, evil, and vile! Now get out of my sight, before I sink my fangs into you. Oh, how I hate kids!"

7

SO JACOB TWO-TWO WAS REMOVED from the lair of The Hooded Fang and led along a winding corridor and down two hundred steps to a row of subterranean cells by Master Fish and Mistress Fowl.

A tearful little boy stuck his head out between the bars of the first cell Jacob Two-Two passed. "Please, sir," he cried to the guards, "please, I've got a terrible tummyache."

"Shall we throw him to the crocs, then?" asked Master Fish.

"No, feed him to the snakes."

"The wolverines are hungrier."

"How do you feel now?" asked Mistress Fowl.

"Oh, much better, thank you, sir," said the boy, retreating from the bars.

A few cells farther down, a little girl's head popped out between the bars. "I'm hungry," she protested. "I'm so hungry."

"Here, then," said Master Fish. "I'll give you a rotten, wormy apple if you promise to eat every piece."

"Ugh," said the girl, retreating.

"What's she in for?" asked Jacob Two-Two. "What's she in for?"

"Why that ungrateful little girl broke out in measles on the very day her father had invited the boss to dinner. Ruined everything."

"You're in the double-security section," said Mistress Fowl. "Only hardened criminals here."

With that, Mistress Fowl unlocked a cell and flung Jacob Two-Two inside. She left him with a jug of water and two slices of stale bread, slamming the barred door.

Jacob Two-Two had hardly adjusted to his surroundings when the entire cellblock was plunged into darkness and a loudspeaker began to crackle.

"Good evening, my little dreadfuls," sang out the menacing voice on the loudspeaker, "I do hope that you've all finished every last delicious drop of your good-night glass of curdled wolverine's milk and that you are all nicely tucked in on your cold, splintery bed boards, with your cell doors firmly locked, because oh, dear, oh, dear, *one of our snakes is missing and is rumored to be slithering through the cellblocks right now in search of some tasty toes.* Well, now, don't worry, because once more it's Happy Nightmare Hour, with your most unlovable Slimer, yours truly, Uncle Oscar Octopus. Last night, if you remember, we left our hateful hero, Dan Disrespectful, fleeing across the haunted swamp, pursued by Wanda Witch and her pack of sewer rats . . ."

Jacob Two-Two held his hands to his ears, shutting out Uncle Oscar Octopus, until he was certain the Happy Nightmare Hour was over. And, quite suddenly, Jacob Two-Two was very hungry. He had forgotten to eat his dinner. His stale bread. Removing his two slices of bread from his tray, Jacob Two-Two was astonished to discover a chocolate bar hidden beneath. I have a friend in the prison, he thought. But who? Who could it be?

8

"PLEASANT DREAMS, KIDDO," had been Mistress Fowl's last
words to Jacob Two-Two, and Jacob Two-Two, his supersonic bleeper secured in his ear, did have pleasant dreams,
in spite of his squalid surroundings. For he knew that tomorrow, or two days after, the leaders of Child Power—the
intrepid Shapiro, followed by the fearless O'Toole—would
begin tracking him.

Jacob Two-Two awakened with a bounce and was actually
singing when a guard called Mr. Fox, an enormous fellow,
wearing a fur coat, scarf, and earmuffs, came to fetch him
and led him to a door marked FREEZER. "You'll have to have
a shower in here," he said, "before we can issue you with a
prison uniform."

When Jacob Two-Two emerged from the shower, trem-
bling with cold, Mr. Fox shoved a towel at him, saying, "Hurry,
I'm prone to chills." Then, narrowing his eyes, he added,
"Hey, you haven't washed behind your ears."

"I have," said Jacob Two-Two. "I have."

"Then what's this?" asked Mr. Fox, plucking out the supersonic bleeper.

"Nothing," said Jacob Two-Two. "Nothing."

"Nothing? Why, look here," said Mr. Fox, holding it to the light, "it's a precious stone. I'll have it, then. Thank you very much."

Jacob Two-Two kicked, he punched, and he bit, but he couldn't recover the supersonic bleeper. Indeed, all he earned for his effort was a bruised cheek, before Mr. Fox gathered him up and flung him back into his cell.

Lying on the stone floor, Jacob Two-Two sobbed. He sobbed and sobbed, until suddenly he realized he was being

foolish, for it didn't matter one bit that Mr. Fox had stolen his bleeper. Child Power would still track it to the hidden prison and set everybody free.

Mr. Fox appeared again. "We're having a party in the dining hall tonight," he said. "You're invited."

Some party. There were no balloons, no loot-bags, and no ice cream. Even so, Jacob Two-Two was delighted to be led finally into the dining hall, if only to enjoy the company of other little people, boys and girls, who, like Jacob Two-Two himself, were still unable to ride a two-wheel bicycle, dial a telephone number, whistle, do joined-up writing, play checkers, or catch a ball. So many of them, too! Jacob Two-Two hadn't realized until now that there were something like two hundred other boys and girls being held in the prison. All of them dressed in itchy, ill-fitting, gray prison uniforms, their faces pale, circles under their eyes, because on Slimers' Isle they never, never saw the sun.

Jacob Two-Two was seated between two other boys, one called Pete, and the other, Oscar. He liked them both immediately. But before he could ask them any questions, a menu was placed before them. It read:

CROCODILE STEAK
or
TART OF DEATH-WATCH BEETLE
ELECTRIC EEL SOUP
or
SNAKEBURGERS
NETTLE PIE

44

"Whatever you do," warned Pete, "don't take the electric eel soup."

"Why?" asked Jacob Two-Two. "Why?"

"Because," said Oscar, "it's shocking."

At another long table, Jacob Two-Two noticed a little boy crying. A girl, maybe four years old, kept calling, "I want my mommy." Oscar looked sad. So did Pete. And Jacob Two-Two was bursting to tell them about his supersonic bleeper and how all their troubles would soon be over, because any day now the leaders of Child Power, the fearless O'Toole and the intrepid Shapiro, would track them down and liberate everybody. But before he could whisper his secret, all the other children began to shriek, some even hiding their eyes, as the dreaded Hooded Fang padded into the dining hall, growling and baring his fangs. Suddenly, The Hooded Fang frowned. "I know my audience," he bellowed. "I've got antennas. There's a little stinker in here somewhere who isn't trembling for me. Would he please stand up?"

Jacob Two-Two was about to rise, but Oscar held him down on one side, and Pete on the other.

"If you're not afraid," Oscar whispered, "you must pretend."

But it was too late. The Hooded Fang was already upon them, glaring down at Jacob Two-Two.

"So it's you, is it, Two-Two? I'll soon fix that. But first," he said, striding to the raised platform at the head of the dining hall, children scattering left and right as he passed, "I must tell all of you why we are here tonight. We are here to honor Mr. Fox and present him with this month's Rotten-to-Children Award. And, furthermore, I must tell you that as Mr. Fox has been so splendidly cruel here, so rough and tough with little brats, he is being promoted. Mr. Fox will be leaving us. He's going to London. Undercover work. An entirely new division." Here The Hooded Fang paused, his smile vile. *"Toy Shop Sabotage."*

Going to London? Heedless of any danger to himself, Jacob Two-Two raced to Mr. Fox's side and tugged urgently at his sleeve. "When are you leaving?" he demanded. "When are you leaving?"

"Why, tonight," said Mr. Fox, beaming as he flashed the supersonic bleeper at Jacob Two-Two, "tonight, right after the party."

"Then give me back my bleeper right now," cried Jacob Two-Two twice.

In reply, Mr. Fox shook with laughter and gave Jacob Two-Two a shove, sending him sprawling.

"I have failed everybody," thought Jacob Two-Two, and that night he wept fresh hot tears on the cold floor of his cell. For now he knew that the fearless O'Toole and the intrepid Shapiro would never, never find him. He was condemned to linger in the hidden prison for two years, two months, two weeks, two days, two hours and two minutes.

47

9

MEANWHILE, IN THE CHILD POWER TENT, under the shade of the copper beech tree, the fearless O'Toole paced the floor, his cape hanging limp. The intrepid Shapiro sat at her desk, holding her head in her hands.

"If you won't say it, I will," said Shapiro. "We're up the creek without a paddle."

"Poor little Jacob Two-Two."

To begin with, the Child Power receiver in the tent had picked up definite bleeps, tracking them to the outskirts of the fog country, when suddenly everything had gone haywire. The signals were lost.

O'Toole searched, Shapiro cogitated, but again and again they came up with nothing.

Then, two days later, the intrepid Shapiro burst in on the fearless O'Toole, enormously excited, and insisted that she had picked up the supersonic bleeps in the West End of London.

"Why, that's crazy," said the fearless O'Toole.

But they had to pursue every lead. And so, off they ran, through Hyde Park, around Piccadilly Circus, and into the gigantic toy shop of Regent Street that had always been their favorite. The fearless O'Toole followed the intrepid Shapiro to the second floor, through a door and into the packing room, where a jolly fat man sang as he fiddled with boxes of jigsaw puzzles. No sooner did the fat man espy the intrepid Shapiro and fearless O'Toole than he leaped back from the boxes, dropping several pieces of jigsaw on the floor.

"I wasn't doing anything wrong," he said quickly.

"But nobody said you were," said the intrepid Shapiro.

The fat man, who wore dark glasses, kept to the shadows. Eyeing the young intruders suspiciously, he sang out, "Care for a sweet?"

The intrepid Shapiro hesitated.

"Here," said the fat man, offering a chocolate to the fearless O'Toole, "have this."

Suddenly, the fearless O'Toole grasped the man's hand and shouted for the intrepid Shapiro. "Look here," he said. "Quick."

It was the supersonic bleeper, set in a ring on the old man's finger.

"Where did you get it?" demanded the intrepid Shapiro.

"Well," said the fat man, "one day, fishing in the Thames, below Richmond, I caught me a lovely plump trout, of all unlikely things, and no sooner did he land on the bank, flipping and flopping, than he coughed up this precious stone. Gorgeous, isn't it?"

The fearless O'Toole's eyes filled with tears. The intrepid Shapiro bit her lip.

"Oh my," the fat man called back after the retreating Infamous Two, "did I say anything to distress you?"

The intrepid Shapiro was too upset to answer.

"Come and visit me again. Ask for me at the door any time. My name is Fox. Mr. Fox. I love children."

Outside, Shapiro said, "Obviously, Jacob Two-Two was drowned while trying to escape."

"Poor Jacob Two-Two," said O'Toole.

10

DAY BY DAY JACOB TWO-TWO grew thinner, in spite of the chocolate bars and occasional bag of gumdrops that continued to turn up so mysteriously in his cell, each time with a note enclosed—

IF YOU WANT MORE OF THE SAME, MUTTON-HEAD,
TAKE MY ADVICE AND TREMBLE WHENEVER THE
HOODED FANG PASSES.

A FRIEND

With Oscar and Pete, members of his work gang, Jacob Two-Two worked very, very hard indeed, mostly at the fog-making workshop attached to the prison. The fog, Jacob Two-Two discovered, was manufactured by the perfidious Slimers to keep the children's prison safely hidden. Other goods made in the prison included—

1. Jigsaw puzzles too complicated to solve.

2. Pinball machines that registered TILT, if you so much as blew on them.

3. Ping-Pong tables with a net bound to collapse the first time it was struck by a ball.

4. No-flow ketchup, guaranteed to stick in the bottle.

5. Blue jeans labeled preshrunk, but manufactured to shrink still more after the first washing.

6. Dentists' drills.

7. Bad-temper pills for teachers and baby-sitters.

8. Shoes made especially for children to outgrow within three months.

9. Rain for picnics.

10. Weeds to ruin swimming holes.

11. Major news stories concocted to break only when they could replace favorite television programs.

The Slimers also turned out KEEP OFF THE GRASS signs by the thousand, giving them away free, and offered special cut-rate to builders who put up apartment buildings where there were ABSOLUTELY NO PETS ALLOWED, not even a tropical fish

tank. In a word, anything to torment little people or get them in trouble with big people who did, in fact, love them.

Day by day, Jacob Two-Two's skin turned gray, like the other prisoners, and there were soon circles under his eyes, for in the hidden children's prison he never, never saw the sun.

Well, not *exactly* never. For once, tramping through the fog with a work gang, he noticed a thin shaft of sunlight penetrating the gloom in a remote clearing. Another day the guards, also catching a glimpse of the sunlight in the clearing, hastily donned their dark glasses and turned their faces the other way, as if the feeble shaft of sunlight was actually a ray of blinding intensity.

"Hurry," cried the guards. "Get to the fog workshop and get up some more fog. Hurry, brats!"

Inside the workshop, Jacob Two-Two and the rest of his work gang were set to feeding coal into the fog-making machines. Faster, faster. And once their shift was done, they were marched past the Fog Control Room. Here, Jacob Two-Two noticed three Slimers hard at work repairing the Control Switch.

"What happened?" asked Jacob Two-Two. "What happened?"

"Some idiot pulled the switch the wrong way and cut the power," said a Slimer, shivering. "Another ten minutes and the wind might have blown our fog away."

All three Slimers shook their heads, appalled.

"We might have been exposed to the sun," said the second Slimer, trembling at the thought.

"A close shave. A very close shave. Now on your way, brat, we shouldn't be telling you any of this."

Jacob Two-Two continued on his way, his manner pensive. Suddenly, he turned to Oscar. "Why can't they stand the sun?" he asked twice.

"Because," said Oscar, "speaking scientifically, any big person who cannot stand little ones also fears the sun."

"Or pets," added Pete.

"Or flowers," said Oscar.

Or even laughter, thought Jacob Two-Two, remembering The Hooded Fang.

11

JACOB TWO-TWO WAS NOT ONLY overworked and hungry most of the time, but he was also in ever-deepening trouble with The Hooded Fang. The Fang, it appeared, had come to detest him more than all the other prisoners.

"That lousy Jacob Two-Two," complained The Hooded Fang bitterly to his wife one night, "will be the end of me. When I pass, he doesn't cower, shiver, or even tremble, but instead puts a hand to his mouth to suppress a giggle."

Mrs. Hooded Fang was outraged. "But hasn't he seen all the signs on the prison grounds, saying you're vile, inhuman, and vicious."

"The little stinker," cried The Hooded Fang, "was brought up not to believe everything he reads. Furthermore, I can't even get him to admit his age. Whenever I ask him how old he is, he says," and here The Hooded Fang mimicked Jacob Two-Two, " 'Why, I'm two plus two plus two years old.' Worse news. He won't answer his cell door *unless I knock two times*."

"Punish him!"

"But no punishment works."

"Have you tried making him eat soup with a fork?"

"I've tried everything. I must break his spirit, you see, and the only way I can do that is to get him to say anything but two. If only I could get him to say one, three, or even sixteen. Sixteen!" exclaimed The Hooded Fang. "That's it!" And he leaped up, knocking over his wife, and charging out of his lair and down the two hundred steps to Jacob Two-Two's cell, remembering to knock two times.

"All right, Jacob Two-Two," said The Hooded Fang, "if you're such a clever little fellow, can you tell me how many legs I've got?"

"Why, two, of course," said Jacob Two-Two. "Why, two, of course."

"Good. First-rate. And now, Jacob Two-Two," said The Hooded Fang, hard put to conceal a fiendish grin, "can you tell me how many suns there are?"

"Aside from me," said Jacob Two-Two twice, "my father has two. Daniel and Noah."

"No, you twerp! Suns. *S-u-n.* Can't you even spell?"

"I'll answer that," said Jacob Two-Two, "I'll answer that, if you tell me how many times two goes into two?"

"Think I'm an idiot, do you? The answer to that," said The Hooded Fang, thrusting out his chest, "is one."

"And that," said Jacob Two-Two twice, "is how many suns we have."

"You're not playing fair! You're cheating."

"I am not! I am not!"

"All right, then, smarty-pants. Tell me how many ounces there are in a pound."

"Why, that's easy. That's easy," said Jacob Two-Two. "There are two times two times two times two ounces in a pound."

Shaking with rage, counting on his fingers, and then removing his shoes to use his toes as well, The Hooded Fang had to admit that Jacob Two-Two was right. "Oh, I hate you," he bellowed. "I could chew you up right here and now."

"But, Mr. Hooded Fang," said Jacob Two-Two, "please, you mustn't be so sad."

"Mustn't I?"

"Because," said Jacob Two-Two, "you, too, can be a two-two."

"What's that, you little twerp?"

"How many sides are there to every story?" asked Jacob Two-Two. "How many sides are there to every story?"

"Two."

"What should every boy learn to stand on?"

"His own two feet."

"And what will it be when it gets dark?"

"Tonight."

"And where will you go tonight?"

"To bed."

"And what will it be when you wake up?"

"Why, tomorrow, of course," said The Hooded Fang, smiling just a little.

"You see, you see," exclaimed Jacob Two-Two, jumping up and down joyously, "it's easy, it's easy. You, too, are a two-two now."

The Hooded Fang's cheeks flared red. He looked like he was going to explode. "All right, then. I've tried everything. And now there's only one thing to do. Tuesday afternoon at two o'clock, *I'm going to feed you to not* one, but two hungry sharks. Ho, ho!"

"Oh no," cried Jacob Two-Two. "Oh no."

"Oh yes," replied The Hooded Fang, "and what's more, I will personally bring you your last meal."

12

FIRST THING NEXT MORNING, Jacob Two-Two huddled with Oscar and Pete in a far corner of the prison workshop and told them of The Hooded Fang's threat.

"What are we going to do?" asked Pete, enormously upset.

"We are going to try to escape," said Jacob Two-Two. "We are going to try to escape."

"That's impossible," said Pete, and he reminded them of the sign they had all seen on first arriving at the hidden prison—

THIS WAY TO SLIMERS' ISLE
FROM WHICH NO BRATS
RETURN

Mindful of passing guards, whispering, Jacob Two-Two told Pete and Oscar of his desperate plan to liberate all the prisoners . . . with the help of the intrepid Shapiro, and the fearless O'Toole, the fabled leaders of Child Power. Pete was skeptical and a little frightened. But Oscar said, "As plans go, it does have the merit of being scientific."

So that night, unobserved in the dining hall, Pete and Oscar helped Jacob Two-Two draft a letter, making two copies of course. It read—

TOP SEKRUT

To: Child Power
Attenshun: Intrepid Shapiro, Fearlus O'Toole

FOR YUR EYEZ ONLY

Hi Fearlus! Greetings Intrepid!

Bad noos. The supersonic bleeper was stolin from me by one Mr. Fox, whooz now in London on a sekrut mishin, doing sabotage in toy shops. Track down Mr. Fox and he can lead yu to us in the hiddin childrenz prisin. But pleaz remember to dress warmly, becauz to get heer yu must travel by car, trane, bus, canoo, helicopter, ox-cart, rickshaw, stiltz, dingy, skiz, kayak, submarine, flying balloon, camil, dogsled, rollerskates, glider and motorcicle.

Something elz. Bring weapons. With all due respect, yu will need them. Signal yur arrival by poizining the crocodials in the waters that surround the prisin. Then remember not to attak until two o'clock by which time,

with the help of Pete and Oscar, I will have rendered
the Slimers helplus.

> Yurs trooly,
> Jacob Two-Two

PS I hope, in my absinz, you have remembered to feed
my hamster, Mr. Harper.
PPS Hurry! Hurry!

"It's a fine letter," said Pete, "but how do we get it delivered? Even if we had stamps, there's no post office on
Slimers' Isle."

Oscar had to agree.

"There's no post office," said Jacob Two-Two twice, "but there *is* The Hooded Fang."

"You mean," asked Pete, astonished, "he's going to deliver your letter?"

"Maybe," said Jacob Two-Two, "just maybe," and behind his back, his fingers were crossed.

13

FOR HIS LAST MEAL, the night before he was to be fed to the sharks, The Hooded Fang brought Two-Two two lamb chops and two desserts, an unheard of feast within the confines of the children's prison. And then, tears filling his eyes, he sat down to watch the doomed child eat. Finally, The Hooded Fang said, "I'll give you one last chance. I'm going to make my most horrible face, and you're going to scream loud enough so that the other kids know you're afraid of me."

"Oh no, I won't! Oh no, I won't!"

"Oh yes, you will!"

"I won't, I won't," said Jacob Two-Two, "because I know your dreadful secret."

The Hooded Fang retreated a step.

"You're not horrible," said Jacob Two-Two two times, "and you're not disgusting, mean, vicious, or vile."

"Sssssssh," said The Hooded Fang, clapping a hand over Jacob Two-Two's mouth as two guards passed outside. "Somebody might hear."

"You admit it, then! You admit it, then!"

"I DO NOT."

"Every time you leave my cell," said Jacob Two-Two twice, "I find a chocolate bar hidden somewhere. Or a bag of gum-drops."

"I don't know what you're talking about. . . ."

"You do! You do!"

"Possibly, they just drop out of my pockets. I have a sweet tooth—I mean, fang—you see."

"You're not evil," said Jacob Two-Two. "You're not evil."

The Hooded Fang bared his sharp, terrifying fangs. He

growled. He grunted. He rolled his eyes. He leaped up and down.

But Jacob Two-Two didn't tremble. Neither did he cower. Instead, he leapt up and down, growled, grunted, and rolled his eyes right back.

"Cheeky! Oh, I never," said The Hooded Fang, indignant. "I—I'm feeding you to the sharks at two o'clock tomorrow afternoon."

"If you lead me out of this cell tomorrow," said Jacob Two-Two, "I'm going to hug you and kiss you. I'm going to hug you and kiss you."

"Oh, God, no! You wouldn't."

"In front of all the guards! In front of all the guards!"

"I hate children! Oh, how I hate children! You'll be the ruin of me."

"Not if we make a deal," said Jacob Two-Two. "Not if we make a deal."

"What sort of a deal?"

"I wish to have a letter delivered immediately to the intrepid Shapiro and the fearless O'Toole."

"Child Power! The Infamous Two! Oh no! Never!"

Which is when Jacob Two-Two bounded into his arms and began to hug and kiss him.

"All right! Okay! But cut out the mushy stuff at once."

14

ONCE HAVING DIGESTED THE CONTENTS of the letter, the intrepid Shapiro and the fearless O'Toole did not hesitate. Swiftly, they shed their clothes and donned the Day-Glo blue jeans, the golden capes, and the T-shirts with *Child Power* emblazoned on the chests. Then they strode to the enormous toy shop on Regent Street, lingering behind at closing time, cleverly concealing themselves behind a counter in the model section.

It soon grew dark, and the hours slipped past, seemingly one second at a time.

"Do you think Jacob Two-Two got it wrong," whispered Shapiro to O'Toole. "After all, he's still a very small boy."

Another hour passed. And then Mr. Fox appeared, his eyes hidden behind dark glasses.

As the leaders of Child Power watched, amazed, Mr. Fox cautiously opened a Tiger Tank model, removed a vital part, and slipped it into another box containing . . . a Spitfire model. He then plucked a piece from the Spitfire kit and dropped it into the Tiger Tank kit, before replacing both boxes on the shelves. Then, laughing out loud, he slipped over to the section where the electric trains and racing-car sets were displayed and began exchanging wires here and there, ruining both sets.

As The Infamous Two watched, aghast to witness such villainy, the nefarious Mr. Fox began to work more quickly. He moved to the counter where the most difficult two-thou-sand-piece jigsaw puzzles were kept and busied himself switching pieces from box to box, making it impossible for a boy or girl to complete either puzzle successfully. Mr. Fox began to work faster, faster, and faster, for a toy saboteur's

work is never done. Removing batteries from toy boxes that promised "batteries included," he slipped wrong-size screws into erector sets and made pinprick holes in kites. He sought out the most complicated model kits, removed the English instructions, and replaced them with sheets written in Japanese. Then he turned to the chemistry sets, switching the labels on tubes. "That ought to make for an explosion or two," he cackled.

So happily immersed was Mr. Fox in his wrongdoing that seconds passed before he noticed that somebody had switched on the lights.

"What's going on here?" he demanded.

Too late. For right before him, in Day-Glo blue jeans, her golden cape flying, stood the intrepid Shapiro.

"Aaargh," cried Mr. Fox, turning to flee.

But his path to the stairs was blocked by the fearless O'Toole, his golden cape flying.

Mr. Fox swerved, he pitched a chemistry set at O'Toole, and clambered over the games counter, seizing a bow and arrow. "Say your prayers, brats," he chortled.

"Ha, ha, ha," laughed Shapiro, doing a backward flip over the costume counter and coming to her feet, broadsword in hand. "Not yet, fatso!"

Ducking a volley of arrows, O'Toole seized a cricket bat, tossed a ball in the air, and swung the bat, hitting the ball straight as a bullet at Mr. Fox.

Then a rubber-suction arrow caught the charging Shapiro

in the forehead, and she reeled backward, stunned.

"And how would you like a taste of the same medicine?" cried Mr. Fox triumphantly to O'Toole.

But before he could fire, the intrepid Shapiro ducked under the magic counter, surfacing to pelt their onrushing tormentor with what seemed like a handful of flour, but was actually sneezing powder.

"Aaach-choo," cried Mr. Fox, bending over double. "Aaach-choo!"

In an instant, Shapiro was at his throat, broadsword in hand.

Quivering with fear, Mr. Fox sank to his knees. "Mercy,"

he pleaded between sneezes. "Mercy. I suffer from high blood pressure. My nerves are shot. I bleed easily."

Shapiro drove the sword tip against the coward's throat.

"You wouldn't harm an old man who wears glasses," cried Mr. Fox.

"We're going to spare you, you wretch," said O'Toole.

"We have other uses for you," said Shapiro.

"Aaach-choo," said Mr. Fox. "Aaach-choo!"

15

MEANWHILE, at the children's prison, Jacob Two-Two had spread the word, and all the prisoners were waiting for the sign.

Waiting, waiting.

Until finally in the afternoon, an especially gloomy afternoon, as Jacob Two-Two stood watch on a balustrade of the hidden prison, staring into the surrounding waters, murky and foul-smelling, he suddenly saw something very odd happen. A crocodile that he had been following with his eye slithered onto the marshy shore, heaved, flipped over on his back, and died. The letter *C* was emblazoned on his stomach. Then another crocodile flipped over, dying, this one still in the water, the letter *H* painted on his stomach.

Soon all the prisoners were gathered on the balustrades, watching in amazement. More and more crocodiles were flipping over, dead, and the letters on their bellies read *R,I,E,L,W,D,O,P.* Properly put together, this could only mean one thing!

"CHILD POWER!" shouted one prisoner after another. "It must be . . ."

". . . The Infamous Two."

"We're going to be rescued!"

Even as they leaped up and down gleefully, the prison alarms sounded, and Slimers, armed with slime guns, took up their positions. Then the man who was supposedly the slimiest Slimer of them all, The Hooded Fang, unwrapped his slime-ball cannon, which commanded the surrounding waters. "This is going to be a massacre," he promised.

On the opposite bank, still unseen through the fog, stood the intrepid Shapiro and the fearless O'Toole, and with them, hands bound behind his back, their guide, the nefarious Mr. Fox. The intrepid Shapiro and the fearless O'Toole were armed only with rubber-suction arrows, cricket bats, slingshots, and broadswords, all from the toy shop on Regent Street.

"Remember," declared O'Toole, "Jacob Two-Two says that we are not to set off in the boat until two o'clock. Or everything is lost."

But what, wondered O'Toole, if Jacob Two-Two fails, as he had promised, to render all the Slimers helpless? What's his plan? Can it work? So much—too much, perhaps—depended on a boy who was still very little.

Who couldn't cut a slice of bread that wasn't a foot thick on one end and thin as a sheet of paper on the other.

Or count the laundry.

Or ride a two-wheel bicycle.

Who had to say everything two times, because nobody ever listened to him.

But who, even now, accompanied by Pete and a stumbling Oscar, was racing through the fog to the fog-making workshop, hiding whenever a platoon of Slimers marched past them.

Finally, Jacob Two-Two slipped through an open door and ran past the furnaces to the Fog Control Room, followed by a breathless Pete and Oscar.

The Control Room was abandoned, as they had hoped.

Jacob Two-Two climbed onto a tabletop and pulled on the Control Switch with all his might. Pete pulled on Jacob Two-Two. Oscar pulled on Pete.

"Pull," cried Jacob Two-Two. "Pull!"

They pulled.

"And again! And again!"

Oscar pulled Pete, Pete pulled Jacob Two-Two, and Jacob Two-Two pulled on the switch handle. They pulled and pulled, until the handle finally sank to its off position.

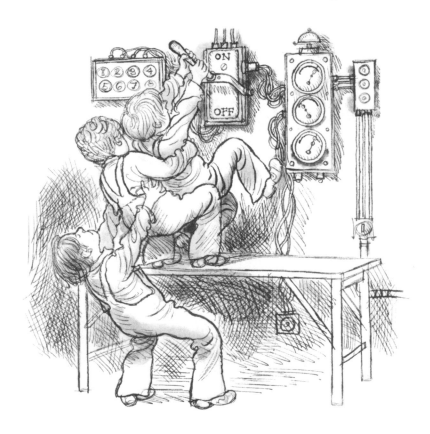

"What do you think, Shapiro?" asked O'Toole.

"It's too late to turn back. We must go forward according to Jacob Two-Two's instructions."

So, at exactly a quarter to two, Shapiro picked up her megaphone. "Hooded Fang," she called out, "we're coming to get you. Surrender while you can. Tell your men to come out with their hands up."

The Hooded Fang answered with a withering burst of slime-ball fire, careful to aim over the children's heads. "Come and get it, you twerps," he hollered.

"Wait! Don't shoot," pleaded a terrified Mr. Fox. "It's me. It's Fox here."

At precisely two o'clock, the leaky rowboat started out across the putrid, fog-bound water, Mr. Fox, his hands untied, bailing water frantically.

Another hail of slime-fire hit the water.

"One more volley," boasted The Hooded Fang, "and the waters will turn red with blood."

But, even as he spoke, a miracle occurred. To everyone's astonishment, the fog began to lift. For the first time within living memory, the sky over the children's prison began to brighten. It grew brighter and brighter, until, lo and behold, there was the sun. The actual sun! The prisoners, overwhelmed, reached out—they stretched their pale arms to touch the sunshine. They cheered, they stamped their feet. "The sun," they cried. "The sun! The sun!"

The Slimers couldn't tolerate it. The sun blinded them, and suddenly they began to stumble and fall. Their slime-guns popped off here and there but always in the wrong direction. The Hooded Fang fired his slime-ball cannon fitfully,

also to no effect, before he retreated, shielding his eyes with his hands. "Put it out," shouted The Hooded Fang. "Somebody please put out the sun!"

The sun grew stronger and stronger. And in the water, sparkling in the sunlight now, the Child Power boat struck for the shore.

"Watch out for the wolverines," cried a prisoner.

But the wolverines, also blinded, tripped and fell over the snakes, and the snakes scurried for the shelter of the darkest, deepest holes on the island. Within minutes, the intrepid Shapiro and the fearless O'Toole, their golden capes flying, were scaling the prison walls. With some help from the prisoners, they easily disarmed and tied up the weeping, blinded Slimers. Then Shapiro and O'Toole sought out Jacob Two-Two.

"You're marvelous," said the intrepid Shapiro.

"Wonderful," said the fearless O'Toole.

"But how did you know the sun would come out at two o'clock?" they both asked at once.

Jacob Two-Two explained that the fog was man-made at the workshop attached to the prison. "All we had to do was throw the switch and cut the power," he said. "All we had to do was throw the switch and cut the power. Big people who hate little ones or pets or flowers or laughter also fear the sun. It blinds them."

Which was when The Hooded Fang himself stumbled

into their midst, still clutching his eyes with his hands. "Put out the sun," he mumbled.

"Don't pay any attention to him," said Jacob Two-Two fondly. "Don't pay any attention to him. He's just pretending."

"Stinker!"

"He's the only one here who doesn't *really* fear the sun," said Pete.

"You know why?" asked Oscar.

"Because The Hooded Fang is childish," cried Jacob Two-Two twice. "He's one of us."

"Oh, I never! I MOST CERTAINLY AM NOT!" shouted The Hooded Fang, peeking at them between his fingers.

"The proof is," cried Jacob Two-Two, "the proof is, whenever he struts across the prison yard, grunting and growling, *he is careful not to step on cracks.*"

"I'm not childish," protested The Hooded Fang, even as he forgot himself so far as to lower his hands and face the sun. "I'm vile! I'm notoriously evil! And if you don't believe it, come to my lair and look at my scrapbook. So there!"

"Empty his pockets," said Jacob Two-Two. "Empty his pockets!"

"No, please! Not that!"

But, even as he protested, The Hooded Fang was seized by the intrepid Shapiro and the fearless O'Toole.

"You're not being fair," complained The Hooded Fang. "It's two against one."

One of The Hooded Fang's pockets yielded a handful of jelly beans and the other, a ball of string, eight rubber bands, three pieces of beach glass, five pebbles, a fountain pen top, and three packages of bubblegum.

Found out, tearful, The Hooded Fang bared his sharp, terrifying fangs. He grunted. He growled.

"You see," said Jacob Two-Two, "you see. He's also funny. He's also funny."

The Hooded Fang burst into tears. "I want my mommy," he wailed.

Everybody laughed. Jacob Two-Two hugged The Hooded Fang. And the next thing Jacob Two-Two knew he found himself in Richmond Park . . .

. . . where weary from his many adventures, he fell asleep.

His father shook him awake. "Jacob Two-Two," he said, beaming, "thank God, you're safe."

"We've been searching for you for hours," said Daniel.

"We looked everywhere," said Noah.

Emma hugged him.

Marfa kissed him and said, "Oh, Jacob."

On the way home, they stopped at the greengrocer's shop. Mr. Cooper was waiting outside, clutching two bags in his hands.

"Don't tell me," he said. "You are Jacob Two-Two. You are two plus two plus two years old. You have two ears and two eyes and two arms and two hands and two legs and two shoes. You also have two brothers and two sisters. And here, if you please, are two pounds of firm, red tomatoes."

"Thank you," said Jacob Two-Two. "Thank you."

His mother was waiting at the door. "Where have you been all this time?" she asked.

Jacob Two-Two told her everything, which only made his mother laugh and say, "Jacob Two-Two, you are too much. You're a dreamer."

A dreamer?

Maybe.

But that night, after Jacob Two-Two had climbed into bed, he was paid a visit by the fearless O'Toole, accompanied by the intrepid Shapiro. They brought him a Child Power uniform that was different from all the others. It contained a pair of Day-Glo blue jeans and a golden cape, but the *Child Power* emblem was emblazoned on the T-shirt two times.

About the Author

MORDECAI RICHLER, Canada's famed novelist, humorist, short-story writer, essayist, critic and script writer, has built his reputation on such works as *The Apprenticeship of Duddy Kravitz* (made into a movie), *St. Urbain's Horseman, Cocksure, The Street, Shovelling Trouble* and other novels and essay collections. Born in Montreal, he has returned there to live after twenty years' expatriate residence in England. His first book for children, full of satirical wit, gentle humor and compassion, is dedicated to his own five children.

About the Artist

FRITZ WEGNER was born in Vienna and has lived in England since 1938. He studied at the St. Martin's School of Art in London where he is now the visiting lecturer in Graphic Design. He has illustrated many children's books, including *The Strange Affair of Adelaide Harris* by Leon Garfield (Pantheon), and stories in *Cricket* magazine. He has also designed several series of commemorative stamps for the General Post Office in England. He lives in London and has four children.